FAE DREAMS & OTHER SCHEMES

FAE DREAMS & OTHER SCHEMES

A Fantasy Short Story Collection

GWEN TOLIOS

Libra Chai

Printed by Libra Chai

Contents

Spell Update

"I don't understand!" Kaiyi wailed, head falling onto the bar. It hit the wood with a *thunk* that made Appson wince. Kaiyi may have a thick skull for a human, but not that thick. He gently padded his friend's back with one of his claws.

"The model units worked *perfectly*," Kaiyi continued, "We tested the automatic tracing feature, the spell library, the voice activation. We tested it with all sorts of facial features too. Fangs. Snouts. Hoarse throats. The software would recognize any spell command, regardless of who spoke it."

"It was good work," Appson agreed. "Very thorough."

Kaiyi ignored him to resume her wailing. "We tested the software upload process too!" She picked up her head as the bartender placed down a refill of her Newton Newt. In three seconds, the highball glass was half empty.

The bartender raised an eye, inquiring about another, but Appson gave a fierce shake of his head. "Can we get a basket of fries?" They'd have to return to the office sooner rather than later. Best to start carbing up.

The man nodded and headed toward the kitchen.

Kaiyi's lament continued, unaware of anything but her misery. "I don't know what went wrong, but I just know I'm gonna get fired. Work was filled with nothing but complaints about witches not getting the update. They've been waiting a year for this and I blew it for the company. We have no idea what went wrong, why, how to fix it-" Kaiyi threw back the second half of her cocktail. "The delivery of the update was on me. They'll want to point fingers at someone. App, I'm gonna lose my job."

Sobbing, she let her head fall back to the bar.

Her phone *bing!*ed, as it had done every five minutes since they settled at the bar. She slid the device to Appson. "You're the better spell engineer. Technology *listens* to you. Turn it off."

"It could just be your mom-"

"Doubt it."

Appson delicately picked up the phone. The model had been designed for human hands, not his larger, clawed variety. He placed the phone on Kaiyi's skin so her magic signature could unlock it. Then, he went searching for the mute setting.

The phone vibrated with an incoming message. A Circles conversation had 68 new messages. Appson winced. They'd only been at the bar thirty minutes but work never stopped. Especially when there was something to debug. Kaiyi's much-needed, non-office, whine time might have to be cut short.

Gritting his teeth, he opened the office app. It wasn't the engineering channel, but a social one. He prepared to close out when a new message caught his eye: a news screenshot.

Appson tapped Kaiyi's arm. "They found out what went wrong."

Her head shot up, alcohol buzz fading away.

He tilted the device, showing off the photo.

ROOMBA SUMMONINGS the headline of a mundane news site read.

"The humans' Roombas updated instead of witches' Broombas."

"Ohmygod." She grabbed her phone, bringing it up to her eye. She had to squint to read. "Do you think I'm still going to get fired?"

"You're not going to get fired," Appson sighed. "It's an honest mistake. And who knows, PR might be able to ride this out. We love making fun of humans and I can see the memes. I'll even make the first one. Now, come on. Can you code? We might not know what the error was, but we know what to look for and where."

Kaiyi slapped silver on the bar, even as she muttered a spell under her breath. One of the charms on her bracelet flared, and then there was the spell engineer Appson knew, dry-eyed and ready to type.

"Yeah. Let's go."

He grabbed the fries and followed her out.

Crystal Advice

Serenity watches as the priestesses carry her mother's body first through the dark tunnels under the castle and then down the steps into the Crystal Bowl, amazed at their sure feet. The way is barely lit and the ground slippery: she's lost her footing at least once and the only thing she's carrying is a ring in her pocket.

Slowly, the four women at the corners of the silk stretcher reach the bottom of the small, earthen bowl positioned directly under the throne room. It's not a long nor steep descent. When Serenity joins them at the bottom, her eyes land on the top step. Candlelight catches on scattered jewels ringing the bowl, the remnants of priestesses going back centuries.

Upon their death, the women are fed into holy fire which condenses them into crystalline items containing their souls. Ranging in color, shape, and size depending on the priestess, each new bit of crystal, each perfectly preserved soul, joins those of her fellow priestesses in lining the Crystal Bowl.

Serenity looks at a particularly large, oblong piece of blue glass. Inside it, she makes out the rough shape of a priestess from long ago, her robes at least a hundred years outdated. It's not Serenity's right to pick it up and whisper a question to the glass, to get an answer from the soul living in it, but any priestess could. Any one of the women carrying her mother's body.

Today, those crystal-locked souls are onlookers, just like the pallbearers. Within glass, human forms turn and twist to follow the living priestesses, to join their sisterhood regardless of their deaths in watching the compression of a royal soul.

At the center of the amphitheater swirls holy fire. Spherical and hovering over the earth, it comes up to Serenity's chin and is as wide as a pregnant mare. The flames snap, but give off no heat and their light barely reaches beyond the steps. Yet it gives off a sense of unmatched power. The closer she steps, the greater Serenity feels the need to fall into silence. No whisper, no harsh breath, should leave her mouth. No step should make a noise. The desire to subjugate herself rises, to sink to her knees, but she refuses. Holy the fireball may be, but she will not allow it to bend her to its worldview.

If the priestesses struggle with the same, they show no indication. But they too are quiet, bowing their heads as they approach the ball of fire, keeping their gazes on the ground as they circle with her mother's body. Five circles they make, and by the end, Serenity gives in. She bows to relieve the pressure on her back.

With no warning, for how could there be a warning in a place that discourages speech, the priestesses dip her mother's stretcher, and her body slides into the ball of heatless fire.

It consumes Serenity's mother, consumes the Queen, and she lets tears fall down her cheek. She doesn't need to say goodbye, her mother isn't gone, but what has left Serenity is seeing her mother smile. Sensing her warmth beside her as they make their daily prayer to the moon. Feeling her fingers tug Serenity's hair to braid it.

The magical fire flares bright and disappears, leaving behind a suspended, clear, red jewel.

Serenity reaches into her pocket for her newly crafted ring. Slips it on her finger. Then she delicately plucks the jewel that had formally been her mother from the air and pushes it into the waiting setting.

Her first advice-jewel. The one she'd love centered on her crown, but the royal crown is filled with jewels from queens who ruled many years ago. Queens who helped rule the kingdom for centuries, whispering advice to their descendants as they sat on the throne.

The only advice Serenity wants is her mother's.

She'll wait twenty-four hours, as the magic requires, for her mother's soul to settle. Then she can whisper her question into the ring and hear her mother's response, just like her mother had listened to Serenity's grandmother.

She comes from a long line of deceased queens who still advise the living, but the question Serenity is most eager to ask, would ask every day, is "Do you know that I love you, Mom?"

And every day, she knows her mom's voice will come from her soul jewel to say "yes".

Imitation

Imitation is the sincerest form of flattery, so humanity tells itself. It's why they look the other way when the caterpillar-like forms of the Zhihona merge into bipedal shapes.

Humanity saved the last of the species from a dying planet, bringing the creatures into their homes. They say cats and dogs pick up personalities from their owners, why wouldn't Zhihonians pick up traits of humanity.

The aliens develop similar communication organs. Eyes for eye contact. Eyebrows for facial expressions. Vocal cords and mouths for talking. And as the Zhihona take new forms, it becomes obvious humanity shouldn't have thought of them as mindless little pets. While they had wiggled around on a dozen legs, they'd learned, and now they quoted humanity back to the humans.

Imitation is the sincerest form of flattery mediocrity can pay to greatness, the Zhihonians say. They are the mediocrity, banished and starved until the better humans saved them.

Humanity accepts this. Mostly.

Because Zhihonians continue to shift. No longer three-feet-tall, odd-looking bipeds with human faces, Zhihonians transform into children. Even with bodies that look like soapy water, reflective and moving with each step or arm wave, they're so human-like that humanity gives them clothes. The family Zhihona is not a pet, they're an adopted alien child. And as human children mimic their parents in mannerisms, sayings, and actions, so too do the Zhihona.

But Zhihonians grow faster than human children and the shapeshifting continues. Three years after their rescue, Zhihonians are identical matches to the adults who took them in.

Newspapers publish stories about children in the company of Zhihonians who are in danger. Zhihonians who bake poisonous treats. Zhihonians who toss kids who don't know how to swim into pools. A Zhihona doesn't know how to care for human children - what is safe, what is not - but it becomes harder and harder to separate the original from the Zhihonian mimic.

Humanity tries to teach the concept of individuality, about picking unique names or fashion styles. Being shape changers, would the Zhihona want to try blue skin? Green hair? Tails?

No, they all say. We want to mimic the greats.

The Zhihona take it one step further. Humans arrive at work five minutes late, only to find their double already performing the task. Parents attempt to pick up children from daycare, only to realize the family Zhihona got there first.

We're being replaced, humanity worries. My kid does not know me from my fake. My spouse didn't realize it wasn't me they went to bed with. My boss fired my doppelganger.

Humans try to distinguish themselves, but each new tattoo is copied in days. Each new hair dye or style is replicated easily.

We're losing our children to them, someone says. My daughter thinks she's playing with me every day, but she's not.

The Zhihonias need to go. The flattery is unneeded, unwanted, but as a few lynch mobs have proved they've shapeshifted further. Their insides are the same. Their DNA is the same. Zhihonians are human. There is no way to tell the difference.

There never will be again.

Accused

I wake up with just enough knowledge in my head that I know I'm in a hospital. Thin bed with metal rails. Thin sheets and a thin blanket and a thin gown tied at my back. I feel thin too.

The procedure does that, the articles say. You feel less than you were, spread out. The missing memories make you hollow. The machines are selective and particular, building a moat around your memory of the crime. The bigger the crime, the larger the moat, the thinner you feel.

Crimes are detailed to the erasure program using a variety of sources. Witness statements. Forensics. Reports. Each item is a flag of what to keep, so the memory of the crime remains pristine. A reminder of what you did, with the ring of lost memories around it a reminder of what it cost.

Staring at the ceiling of my hospital room, I know this happened to me. I've committed a crime. Memories have been erased as punishment. There is no other reason for me to be here like this, feeling this. I search my mind, looking back and back and back, but there's nothing. No memories of last week, last year. No birthday parties, no smiling grandmas, no trips to the zoo, or a face to match the ring on my left hand.

There's absolutely nothing.

Including a crime.

The detailed situation the machines were told to ignore hadn't existed in my head, and now all I'm left with is a body covered in liver spots and a lifetime I can't recall.

Super Clean

EXPRESS CLEANING! Your ad reads. YOUR WHOLE HOUSE HOLIDAY READY IN 30 MINUTES.

You charge $500, which isn't that steep. Regular housekeepers charge $250 to $300, and you are offering added benefits. You truly offer express cleaning. Some houses you can do in under twenty minutes. A studio apartment takes one.

Your power of automatically cleaning a room as soon as you walk into it isn't flashy like flying or super strength, but it's pretty profitable. It grows on you.

Your business expands. You've attracted a clientele of celebrities who pay you to walk through their house daily, dentist offices that like how your powers will also sterilize instruments, and city governments who turn clean train stations into a tourist marketing campaign. You make money walking. Life has never been so good.

The more people want you, the more you charge. Most don't hesitate at the cost, thrilled to have something sparkling quickly.

A building management company calls. They own three skyscrapers in the city, each with over sixty floors and thousands of rooms. Every night, they want you to walk into each of them.

It's a lot of rooms and a lot of time, but they're offering more money than you make from your current list of clients and so you consider it. It's just strolling the same route night after night, after all, and they're even offering a driver to ferry you between buildings.

You ask to explore the buildings first - learn a potential walk path, judge the timing - and show up unannounced to get a sense of how dirty the building can get. More dirt = more energy use on your side. Thousands of rooms nightly might get exhausting quickly.

Googling clients isn't something you do - working for the celebrity market brings up a lot of false information - but you wonder if maybe you should have in this case. When you show up, there's a picket line.

A picket line of cleaning staff.

You talk to them, stomach sinking as you start to piece together the offer you're considering. The building management is willing to give you money, *a lot of money*, but it's still cheaper than meeting the demands of the third-shift cleaners. Many spend their own money on rubber gloves. They require better health care, considering how many chemicals they inhale daily. PTO is non-existent.

Taking this job deprives two dozen people of theirs and you can't do it. You already make good money - your job is easy and people pay well. You don't need *more*. But these people do.

You're no superhero, but you are a super cleaner. If the

trashy things in the world are CEOs, well, it's suddenly your job to take them out.

You turn down the building management company's offer. You keep your rich clientele. And you funnel the proceeds into labor rights lobbyists.

Cassandra Dreams

It's the waiting that gets to her. Knowing what she knows, and waiting for others to discover the same facts. Waiting for her dreams to come true, for the images of blue lips and clawed torsos or sleeping children to not just live in her head. For them to become stuck in someone else's brain too, nightmares and thoughts and flashes of bodies circling round and round in a loop

The longer it takes, the more pressure builds in her body. Her lungs are full of words she cannot say, her heart pained as the release she wants is blocked, her brain dizzy with anxiety as she waits for the world to *know know know.*

And then there it is. Small little paragraphs, maybe a sentence. Police reports. Obituaries.

She's not the only one who knows they've passed. The only one who has seen the mutilated bodies, or the stiff hands, disarrayed hair on a pillow. The heaviness of being the sole owner of that knowledge fades away.

It'll hit her again the next time she dreams.

Transfae

Most people don't notice the change originally. They think they have turned over a new leaf: being kind. They show up to a birthday party of a friend they didn't want to attend but had given a halfhearted promise to show up at and decided day of they might as well. They promise not have a drop as DD, and don't. Promise to extend a child's bedtime by thirty minutes and find they don't have the heart to flip off the light at 8pm. If they didn't keep their promise, they would be a liar. And no one likes a liar.

Everyone turns over that same, new leaf.

Things get weird on the nightly news. Anchors choke reading the teleprompter. One, it's nerves. A hundred and twenty anchors in local markets, all owned by the same company, choking on the same line? They choke and turn to their co-hosts and the news switches to commercials. The compilation videos go viral.

It's someone's personal blog that leaks the script. It contains a video of them trying to read the transcript. They choke like the anchors. Same spot. But they force themselves through the whole three hundred words, learning when to stop trying and skip the sentence. It's followed by the text of the script, each line they couldn't say highlighted in red.

The internet takes twelve hours to realize that each red line is a lie.

What follows is a flurry of experiments. Personal. Public. On social media. In labs. On live TV. In private recording booths for podcasts. As time goes on, restrictions get worse. Broader. It spreads from America to Canada to Brazil to Nigeria to Ukraine to Nepal.

The human race can't lie, not vocally, and eventually not via the written word either. Erroneous facts are unable to fall from a person's mouth, and people are physically compelled to ensure something they said they'd do is done. Not doing it would have made the statement a lie, after all.

When the first politician collapses, the world learns past promises will catch up to you. 'Empty promises' are a thing of the past.

Everyone thinks before they speak. Science takes on more weight. More experiments are run – where is the border between fact and opinion? It's already been determined that even if you don't know something is factually wrong, you still can't say it. But what about something with no proof either way?

The Lord's Prayer remains intact – *I believe in one God.* The Bible does not – *In the beginning God created the heaven and the earth.*

No one needs to prosecute companies for false advertising anymore – they're self-policing. Lying court witnesses are quickly spotted.

Then comes a grad student's thesis. While the world has

been looking forward, understanding the limits humanity suddenly found themselves bound to, three students looked back. They asked themselves 'why' and scoured the internet and conducted interviews to trace the spread of honesty. Who was bound to the truth first?

The answer is the parents of Sara Connelly.

"I found a sparkly thing in the creek," Sara Connelly says first to her parents, then the students, and eventually international news sources. "And then I made a wish on it."

"And what was that wish?"

"I wanted to be a faerie. And I wanted everyone else to be faeries too."

"Do you know what the sparkly thing was?"

"A rock? I don't know. I threw it back in the water. Like you throw pennies in a wishing well. The water took it away."

Once the curse of honesty stretches around the globe, new changes appear. Cast iron skillets disappear from stores, while sales of protective equipment sore. Old wrought iron fences are torn down, or covered in pool noodles at key points.

With each generation, humanity gets sharper teeth, pointier ears, and starts to shrink.

Sara makes news again showing off her granddaughter's wings.

A Hand For Sticks

I sit on the steps to what remains of my altar, head in my hand. "I used to be a god, you know."

Dog says nothing, just wags his tail as he noses the stick forward. It's not very large, and he's chewed the bark off completely.

I grab it, and with an immense amount of effort, toss it across the temple. Dog chases after it, leaping over roots.

Reduced to tossing sticks. How banal. Years ago, the people of this area would ask for more. Clearings in the forests for farms, twisted and woven branches for homes. I'd moved trees, earth, and bedrock because it made them happy.

The more they wanted, the more I could do.

My believers grew in number and I grew in power. They built my temple without my help, a gift and proof of their devotion. It used to shine with loyalty and love. Now it reeks of abandonment and I cannot get rid of the grime.

Dog comes back, slobbering on the stick. He drops it on my step. I pick the stick up, pat his head, and throw it again. It hits an oil basin, spinning out of sight, and Dog barks happily as he gives chase.

I don't have legs today. Sometimes I do when Dog wants a

walk, but he's quite capable of exploring himself. But he needs someone with hands to toss sticks so I sit here, my lower half a mess of broken, moss-covered rocks, and use sapling-thin arms to give Dog what he wants.

I used to be tall because that was expected of a god. Powerful, because that was also desired. But they'd only believed me powerful in certain aspects, and thus also imagined aspects where I was weak. They saw how much damage that first attack of fire did. They did not come to me for help, not thinking I could, and thus I couldn't. My woods burned.

They saw me as weak, and so I was. They determined me to no longer be worthy of worship, and so I wasn't. I wasn't anything for very, very long.

Across the temple, Dog barks. He's abandoned the stick for a small critter scampering over a fallen wall. His desire for me diminishes. My arms disappear.

"Dog!" I call out.

He turns to look at me, his expectation to see me means I can stay here on the altar for the next ten minutes. What Dog wants of me, I give him.

But what I want, he gives me too.

Existence.

I Wish I Could

Henry rolls over as soon as the alarm rings to face me. "I'm in a time loop."

"Okay," I say.

Henry likes to joke, and this would be something similar to stuff he's pulled in the past, but there's something off about how he says it. How he looks. Despite us going to bed early last night, he's exhausted. Haunted.

"What do you want to do about it?"

He stares at me, love seeping into his gaze even as he gives me a sad smile.

"Can we just... lay here? It'll all reset anyway, no matter what I do. I just... I can't do it right now. I can't, Amiee."

"Then you won't." I brush away the hair falling into his eyes. "I'll email my boss, tell her I caught Covid. Then I'll pick up a box of cookies from the bakery, and we can stay in bed all day eating them. Maybe watch Netflix."

Henry snakes his arms around me, pulling me close. His head dips onto my shoulders, his left leg pinning both of mine. He used to do the same to body pillows until I convinced him I was a much better hold.

"Or," I whispered, running a hand down his back gently. "We can just curl up and nap today."

"I'll let you go in a minute. I just. It's just. Yes, cookies sound wonderful. Thanks. For believing me. Suggesting that."

I pull back to kiss him, soft as butter. "Of course. I love you, and you obviously need a self-care day. Or an Amiee-care day."

"I love you so much," he says. "I wish I could marry you."

I kiss him again, not liking the sound of that. Why couldn't he marry me? I ignore the accompanying thoughts and reach for my phone. I have an email and bakery order to place.

The Human Choice

You know you're not supposed to take candy from strangers, but there's something about the woman on the park bench. The giant bag of jellybeans on her lap. Her long, blued hair. Every time you turn your head away, it cranes back around.

She's not pretty or ugly. Old nor young. She just stares at you, and each time you catch her eyes she smiles, patting the bag of candy with one hand and beckoning you toward her. It's so over the top that you honestly believe she just wants to give you candy. She can't be a kidnapper. She's too obvious.

You nudge your twin. "Come with me to talk to her?"

Julie looks at you with confusion. "Talk to who?"

"The..." You trail off as you watch a young girl skip ahead of her parents, right past the woman. She doesn't offer the jelly beans. The family doesn't turn their head. In a crowded park, she has a whole bench to herself. You wonder if you're the only one who can see her. "Never mind. I'll be right back."

"Make it quick, Julia. I want you to watch me beat Conner's butt at chicken." She bounces on her toes, eyeing the monkey bars.

You grin at your twin, then scamper across the grass. Up

close, there's something visually wrong with the woman: long thin fingers, too big eyes, a narrow face, and a torso that doesn't look as wide as it should be. You know from the few horror movies you've snuck a peek at you should be worried. But as much as this woman doesn't look human, she also feels right.

"Your thirteenth birthday is in a week," the woman says. It sounds like the movie quotes you and Julie garble at each other while brushing your teeth, trying to be clear around plastic and toothpaste foam. Yet it sounds so right in your ear you almost wonder if the entire city just learned to speak wrong.

"Do you want to celebrate by returning home?"

You don't understand. "Our birthday party is at the house?"

The woman smiles. Her teeth are filed one moment, blunt the next. "That house is not your home."

She dips her hand in the jellybean bag, but it's not candy she pulls out. It's a plant. She holds it between her fingers, palm down, and you put out your hand to catch it.

Your skin tingles as soon as the leaves touch. You stare as your hand shimmers, the fingers getting longer, thinner, as your palm shrinks. With a yelp, you drop the clover.

Your skin continues to tingle but reverts to its normal appearance.

It's *human* appearance. This woman isn't human, and you have a sinking feeling you aren't either. You pull your hands to your chest, scared.

"There's a place for us," she says. "Where you can be your true self."

You look back at the playscape where Julie is taunting

Conner. It's always been you two. Julie and Julia, twins for-ever. Sharing plates of spaghetti, sitting nestled between their parents on the couch for movie night. You have a dresser drawer filled with your favorite shirts, a toy bin full of cos-tumes you love to wear, an album of birthday cakes.

Nothing about your life feels *untrue*. Except you now know you're not human.

No one else needs to know that. You were raised human. You can continue to be human. Continue to be Julie's twin, your parents' two-minute younger daughter. *That's* your true self.

"No," you tell the woman. "My place is here."

You run back to the playground just as Julie wraps her hand around the monkey bar to cheer on your sister.

Undine's Child

Her watermark was creeping down her legs. Each day, another scale. She slathered lotion on, hoping to prevent the itch as it replaced skin. She showered daily, seeking the soothing sense of water.

Her dad had warned her, going to college so far from saltwater might be a problem. She'd dismissed it. Surely, she could spend a semester away from the ocean.

And she had, her first year. And her second. But her first scales showed before Thanksgiving this year, easy to keep hidden under her jeans, until a swim over Christmas break at home washed them away. Now, she had a month left of classes in the spring semester, and her scales would soon peak out of her capris.

They always started on the back of her thighs; hard to see, hard to scratch. Better than her hips, where they would chafe against waistbands or other more obvious places like her hands or face. There was a lot of space on her thighs, and they were easy to hide, but they'd hit the top of her calves this morning. In her dream world, the scales would move around her leg and not down it, but they always progressed steadily down the back of her legs in a thin band one, maybe one and a half, inches wide as they rushed to overtake her most human feature – her feet.

Spraying saltwater on them hadn't worked. Nor soaking in a salt bath. She needed the ocean, but she needed to pass her classes. Needed her degree.

Give me five weeks, she prayed. *Five weeks to hide what I am.*

And then the summer to figure out how to deal with them for all of next year.

Play On

"Were you born a girl or a boy?"

I've been asked a lot of stupid, ignorant questions in my life. Most of the time, I recognize they come from a place of ignorance and try to help people crawl out of that hole. Better they get an answer from the source, yeah?

But *this* question. If it comes from anyone over thirteen, it grates.

"Neither," I say. "They evicted me from my mother's body."

Technically true. I was a caesarian birth; the doctor ripped me from the womb like a hacker home manager realizing a tenant had run out of money. I can tell immediately I gave the wrong answer.

The ref crosses himself and steps back. He's one of *those* people. I wish people wore their religion as openly as their gender. I got called demon-child a lot when younger, for different reasons of course, but there is something darkly humorous about being the reason someone crosses themselves.

The ref pushes on, insistent on getting the 'right' answer before allowing the game to start. "What were you born as?"

"A human."

He's getting riled. A nasty thing, as the ref's vexation could spill over from me to my teammates. Am I setting up my team to get more whistles, lose borderline calls, and be open to fouls from the other team with no consequences? Will my comebacks prevent us from winning today and heading to regionals?

"What does your birth certificate say?"

I puff up, indignant. This is not the time nor the place, but I can't help it. He's not looking for understanding. He's not genuinely curious. He has his opinions, wants me to prove him right, and he plans to use that to force me away from something I've strived for all year.

My parents don't have the right to define me. This referee less so.

"What are you?" he hisses.

I'm an aggressive player. I use my height and bulk to my advantage on the soccer field and my mouth to my advantage off of it. Being sassy is how I protect myself. And right now, though I shouldn't, I know I'm going to say something to make the next 90 minutes of my team's life hell.

"Something wrong?" A voice calls out. Amy Russo, the team's trainer, walks behind the goal line toward us.

"Your player is not allowed to play."

I stiffen. I've been tossed out of games before, but not this season. Everything has been straightened out with the district. But, I remember, these aren't our normal referees. They swap at the end of the season to avoid potential bias as teams move from district to regional to state championship games.

I panic. At higher levels, will my place on the team, in the sport, be contested every game?

"Why not?" Amy says, crossing her arms and curling a clipboard to her chest.

It's not uncommon for keepers to have conversations with the refs before kickoff. Quick equipment checks of the goalie and the net. Our talk has been long enough to attract attention.

The other twenty-one starting players on the field are looking at us. Parents on the bleachers are muttering. The sideline referees stare too.

"This is a girls' team." The ref says, noticeably glancing towards my lack of breasts.

I want to snap a lot of things at him. That I am a girl, inside. That he is letting stupid physical stereotypes get in the way. That I take after my dad. Cock my hip, batter my eyelashes, swish my ponytail. Or just say the most sarcastic "duh" in the world.

This team has fought on my behalf for years. Against students, parents, teachers, boards. Dealt with the punishments. Threw a few punches. They know when to step in to prevent my mouth from getting us all in trouble.

Amy answers the ref before I can.

"I've got her medical records and other necessary paperwork in my bag. Everyone on this field, everyone on the bleachers, *from both teams,* knows she's allowed to play and expects to see her out here." Amy glares at the ref from behind the goal line, daring him to ask her to whip them out. No doubt, that's exactly what's on her clipboard.

Everyone knows about me. It caused a hullaballoo in all six towns in the district, after all.

It's a blessing and a curse.

Today, it's a blessing.

"Does the district —"

Amy cuts off the ref with a snarl. *She got state approval.*

The ref frowns.

Amy continues. "If you pull her from the game, you're overturning a decision of the state board on a whim. Pretty sure that's a career killer."

The ref's frown sags further until he's pouting, but he backs down. He probably has heard of me but thought he could push and get his way. Almost did too. If I had continued backtalking, he would have been in his rights to card me.

I look at Amy. The trainer stands with her fists on her hips, glaring with all the power of a large, local campaign donor. She's beautiful and brilliant. "Start. The. Game."

The ref stands tall. "I can't until you're no longer behind the field. It's a safety concern."

Amy looks at me. I feel like if I talk, something might slip around my tongue to take back all the help she's just given me. I smile and pop in my mouthguard.

It's bright pink and clashes horribly with my maroon shirt, but oh well.

Amy looks towards the bench, from where Coach Bart and the non-starters watch us. Coach taps his watch and gestures to the center circle.

The ref grumbles but trots away.

"Lob a ball at his face," Amy says before jogging back to the sideline.

I spend a moment debating if the trouble would be worth it, I've already pushed the referee toward the other team's favor, but then the whistle blows and we have to defend against a kickoff.

I can think about how angry I am later.

For now, I have to concentrate on protecting the net.

A Feathered Master

He had limits to his powers, all genies did, but today he discovered a new one: he could only grant wishes to those he understood.

Normally, language problems weren't an issue. English, Greek, or Amharic, the magic in the lamp translated spoken word for him and his master.

What it didn't translate was bird.

He floated there, three inches high, as he watched the robin. His lamp, an old porcelain sugar bowl, had wound up on a fat windowsill. Someone had to have put him there, maybe as a rain catcher or future succulent vase. They had to have been wearing gloves, to have not woken him when they removed the bowl's lid.

And then they left his lamp to the birds.

As he watched, the robin's tail brushed against the bowl as he hopped along the edge of the wide sill, inspecting the backyard. It chirped and took to the air. He didn't go far, flying up to inspect the overhang of the window. In a drizzle, it'd shelter half the window sill. Including the sugar bowl.

The robin landed on the edge of the sugar bowl and peered inside.

"Oh, no. Don't. I live there!" Where was the matching lid? Surely he had enough power to drop it into place?

Too late. The robin settled into the bowl. It wiggled around, peeped, then flew off.

The genie watched it go. The magic of his creation stated anyone who rubbed his lamp to wake him would be his master, so he was now tied to the bird as surely as he was tied to his lamp. A lamp that came with a tether. The robin was probably on his migration and wouldn't return. It meant the genie was stuck awake and staring at the city until someone else claimed his power or the bird died.

#####

The robin came back, again and again. Dry grass, bunches of hair, tiny twigs. In no time at all, his home had become a bird's nest and the genie was doomed to float beside it, awaiting three wishes he would never be able to grant.

The robin ignored him. He wasn't sure the bird could see him, but the chirps and peeps kept him company. One robin became two as their nest became a home, and soon enough three blue eggs were at the bottom of the sugar bowl.

Even if his feathered master couldn't make wishes, the genie still had access to his power.

A nudge here for good weather, another to hide the nest from local predators. He laid a charm that convinced the couple in the house to not open the window until the nest was empty. He kept the birds warm at night, gently nudged the parents to soft, wet spots for easy worm hunting. He started helping the humans too, cleaning dirty dishes, watering the plants.

Normally the restrictions of being a genie – power in exchange for servanthood – would prevent such magic. He wasn't sure if it was permissible because the robin was incapable of making a wish, or because each spell, in a roundabout way, benefited the robin family. Never had the genie used such an amount of magic for a master, built up via small, constant bursts of magical aid.

It was nice, serving because he wanted to versus being commanded. He hadn't realized how much of his free will he'd lost.

Summer came, and the genie knew his time with his robin master would soon end. While he could, he cast a few more spells. That the humans wouldn't disturb his lamp. A luck spell on the robin, his wife, and three chicks.

Hopefully one of them would return next spring.

Given Name

The bump on the Quad was rough, a shoulder-to-shoulder collision. I rocked back on my feet, startled out of Reddit, and found the person in front of me unaffected. They stood on the sidewalk, coffee in hand. There wasn't even a brown liquid spill on their fingers.

"Sorry, how rude of me." They smiled, wearing a mix of a basketball tee and hot pants. Long hair tied back with a ribbon, chunky watch on their wrist. Non-conforming in not just gender, but fashion trends.

I bit back my jealousy. There was no reason for it. "It's cool." I shrugged, "My fault anyway, I was staring at my phone."

I tried to go around them, but they stepped just a bit to the right to block me.

"No, it's my fault," they said. "I could have stepped out of the way and let you hit me instead. Let me get you a coffee for the trouble."

"Nah, I'm good."

"Please, I insist."

"Don't worry about it."

"Well, at least give me your name so I can apologize properly."

They smiled; the stretch of their lips oddly wide. Their teeth were almost too white. As I spoke my name, I felt it fly from my lips, slip between their teeth, and slide down their throat. They swallowed, and suddenly the person before me was who I'd previously been.

Their smile fell, they stared at their chest, and while I was, had been, intimately familiar with the horror on their face, all I could concentrate on was how free I felt.

For years, my name caused issues. Masculine and oppressive, it bound me from an early age. The need to live up to it, in statute, in success, in form and in society that always chased me fled as surely as my name. I wore Hermes's shoes, wings on my feet eager to take me wherever I wanted.

The park, where no one knew me to judge my dance. The admin building, where changing majors would not come with crippling guilt. Downtown, to try on dresses. Home, where I could declare a new name, a feminine name, and start laying down the cobblestones for a path that others could follow.

"I changed my mind," the person before me said. "I don't want your name."

"You asked for it," I said, "I accept your apology for the shoulder bruise."

I turned on my heel and walked away, already brainstorming the perfect, new name.

Star Chaser

Joey plucks the purple flower petal and chews it. He knows they're more potent when dried within a circle of mustard seed, but all he has around him are fresh blooms and he needs the stamina. Needs the energy to stumble back home.

He should have checked the star chart. He could have made sure to have a pill on him.

Joey stares up at the sky. Dawn is breaking, but the night is dark enough he can see stars and the remnants of a meteor shower. A shooting star streaks across the sky, and something in Joey's chest moves in a similar path, rushing from one side of his body to another so violently his right arm flings out as if to catch the star in his palm before it hits the horizon.

He doesn't, of course. He's in a field of wildflowers and the stars are thousands of miles above his head. His feet ache, a testament to how far his body walked while his mind napped. The energy from the petals is slowly flowing through his blood, even as Joey uproots another flower to eat.

Properly prepared, the power of three flowers would have gotten him home. Restricted to fresh supplies from newly bloomed plants, he'll have to eat twenty.

He chews petal after petal, thankful he's not a goat because they taste awful. He wishes he could swallow them whole, but knows he needs to grind each petal with his molars.

Another star streaks across the sky, but it's harder to see as the sun's rays creep over the horizon. The pull in his body is less too, no flung arm, but he can't help the shift of his shoulders as his sternum follows the meteor's path.

He rips up another flower and grinds.

The ache in his body slowly fades, just as the stars are, just as the night is, just as the sense of not being in control of his limbs transitions into full ownership. With the morning birdsong comes the strength and will to push himself to his feet.

He should have checked the star chart; this happens every time there's a meteor shower and he could have prepared. At least today he can see the mountains on the horizon and figure out due north. At least he's still in the valley.

Joey climbs up a nearby hill and sees landmarks he recognizes. It's a long walk back to his cottage. Six, seven hours. He'll lose a day of work, only to arrive exhausted and starved.

Joey starts walking, filling his pockets with purple blooms as he goes. He'll need the energy.

Post-Mortem Project

Being dead sucks enough that I quickly search for a medium. There's only so long you can haunt the world before your unfinished business itches in your soul and you need it done so you can move on. Finding one is hard, but eventually while flying over rural Indiana I see a house flare with purple lights. The neon is for the living, the aura is for me.

I float through the roof and startle her in the kitchen, pouring herself a gin and tonic. The oven clock reads 14:24, but I'm not one to judge. I plan to wait for her to finish stirring before talking, but she surprises me.

"Unfinished business or contact with a loved one?" she asks, dropping the spoon in the sink and turning toward me. She's youngish, but there's no ring on her hand. Mid-twenties. Thirty if she religiously uses retinol. Large gold hoops hang from her ears, but otherwise, she is in jeans and a light sweater. No one on the street would peg her for a medium, but then again, before I died I thought all fortune tellers and their ilk wore long robes and lots of rings.

To my ghost sense, she glows purple. "Unfinished business."

"Sure, I'll help." Ms. Medium says before I even finish.

"You don't even know what I need."

"You need my help to move on, yeah? I have to help. It's like, the medium Hippocratic oath. Help ghosts. Unless your unfinished business is murder." She takes a sip of her cocktail. "Is it murder?"

I shake my head. "It's finishing a project for my niece."

"Awwww." She melts, and if I were alive, I would be forced to show photos. "What's the project?"

"Well..." I need it done, to scratch my itch and move on to whatever there is to move on *to*. But it's such an oddly specific thing that I'm embarrassed to ask. Could I stay on Earth for another month? Do I really want this medium to help? Could I find another? Can she even do it?

"Look, you're already here." Ms. Medium flicks her hand through the air. "I said I'd help. It can't be that bad."

"I'm recording every Dr. Seuss book for her."

"Kay."

"In a Donald Duck accent. Because he's her favorite."

The medium blinks. "Yeah, you're gonna have to possess me for that one because I will not be able to do it without cracking up."

"But you can do it?"

"Let you possess me so you can record stuff? Heck yeah." She slams back the rest of her gin and tonic. "Tell me what books you have left to do, and I'll grab copies today."

Siren Screech

Above the sound of screams, fear from sailors and delight from your family. Above the sound of cracking wood. Above the sound of waves and seagulls and the soft rattle of your chain and the rasp of your voice. Above it all you hear a faint shout.

"Stop! Stop!"

You stop, looking around your little island, and see a sailor. He's soaking wet, clinking to a rock. There's a cut above his forehead, and as you stare at him a large wave splashes in his face, wiping away the trail of red.

"Stop!" he pleads again, knowing he's gotten your attention.

You stare at him, considering.

Your singing is bad, you know this. It's bad because it's evil, luring ships to their doom. But it's also bad because it's never been a talent you've fostered. And why would you? An awful voice can lure a ship to its doom just as well as a melodious one. Sometimes quicker, the sound drives sailors mad, makes them willing to do anything to get the sound to stop. If they drown trying to get to the riches they think you have or bash their skulls on the mast in madness, does it matter?

It's blood and bodies either way.

But no one has survived before. No one has swum to your island, climbed the slick rocks, and looked at you.

He pulls himself out of the water and staggers toward you.

He doesn't seem to notice your condition. The dryness of your scales. The chapped nature of your lips. It rains too frequently for you to dry out, but you are as ugly as your voice.

You open your mouth to continue singing. There are others still struggling in the waves. This sailor will feel the buzz of madness, the screech of pain in his ears.

"Please stop!" He shouts, killing the sound in your throat.

He's feet away, breathing heavily from pain and exhaustion and there are tears in his eyes. Saltwater drops to add to the sea.

"You're a seagull! An albatross! I have never heard something so horrid in my life!"

There's something off about the sound. An accent to his vowels, a slurring of the words. It's as if he doesn't know what speech should sound like, and you realize that's correct.

The sailor is deaf.

"It's horrid," he repeats, crying and smiling, "but I can hear it. It's also killing the crew, so please stop."

Behind him, the last swimmer goes under and you watch the ship split on the rocks. Shipfall. Below your pod is feasting, ripping legs apart and collecting treasure. If you are lucky, one of them will bring you the nibbled remains of an arm. Maybe a broken toy to keep you company. You have twenty more years chained to this island.

You can understand the humans' language, but cannot speak it. Not with gills pressed flat against your neck. Not with pointy teeth. You never sing human words, but they translate all the same because sirens speak to human hearts.

So you sing to this one's. Just as bad, but softer. You don't need a ship to hear you. You aren't broadcasting to thirty hearts, just one.

"Unchain me and I will sing to you every day. You will hear speech and I will feel the water. We can talk daily. You will hear."

You flip your tail around, show off the rope made of kelp and coral and rusted chains. He reaches for a knife in his boot and slashes at the kelp, stomps on the coral, and there's enough gap in the chain for you to wiggle free.

He looks at you as if you're his heart's desire, and it's true. You have not stopped singing that.

But you have your own desires.

Freedom and food, of which you now have both.

Four Weeks

Everyone laughs and thinks it's a coincidence. You do have a very common name, after all. You share it with at least two celebrities and what must be thousands of people. Everything else in the capsule is a snapshot of fifty years ago, items to share around and laugh over. But this one might be personal. This one might be more than magazine clippings and stale candy. Still, the history teacher who dug up the time capsule passes you the note.

People lean in, confirm yes, that's your name, and then comes the barrage of comments to open it.

On the thick paper is a single handwritten line. *Get your affairs in order.*

Your classmates are confused, and you pretend to be confused as well before suggesting it's a weird prank from the past. Someone guessed that someone with your name would be here, and with a name like Jennifer Johnson, it's a good guess.

People buy it, which is what matters. Because you know the truth; the letter *is* for you. For you to act on or pass along, you don't know, but you'd know your mother's handwriting anywhere. She writes Jennifer the same way on every birthday card you receive, on every wrapped Christmas gift, on every list of chores. Your mother wrote this letter and addressed the envelope.

You give it to her when you get home, watch her face as she looks at the envelope. She does her best to blank her face, but you've known your mother all your life. You can tell she recognizes the handwriting as hers. You can tell there's no freakout she's hiding behind pressed lips. And when she reads the letter inside, the slight slump to her shoulders is unexpectedly resigned.

"Mom?"

She doesn't answer, just kisses your forehead. Her lips linger. "What time is your dad home today?"

"I don't know."

"Kay. I have some stuff to do, why don't you order pizza for a 6:30 pickup. You can take the car."

Normally, you love pizza. And normally, you love any excuse to drive. But there's something in your mom's tone you don't like. It's preoccupation. It's sadness. It's the belief that the 50-year-old note is advice she should follow.

You don't want to get pizza. You want to curl in her lap on the couch, cling as tight as you can. But your mom is already walking away, fingering the edge of the letter. You set up shop in the middle of the house to do your homework and don't put in headphones.

You listen to the sound of your mom in the kitchen. Her steps on the stairs. Her voice as she gives you her credit card and says to drive safe. You memorize it all, you photograph every single moment, and you're glad you had the foreknowledge to do so.

Four weeks later, she's gone.

You Won't Find Comfort Here

When you leave, I want you to kill me.

With the same certainty I have of my love for you, I know that you do not feel the same way. I'm a distraction, a rebound, a look-a-like to your dearly departed, and you will never be completely mine.

But I am yours. I can't think of anyone else I would embrace in this manner, anyone else whose arms I crave. I am yours and do not wish to connect with another once you leave.

I don't ask for your heart, I know I can't have it, but perhaps a piece of your mind? Where you think of me from time to time fondly and remember my touches upon your skin. Where you say my name instead of theirs. Tell some stranger of me, and not *him*.

You ended when they died, just as surely as I will end when you leave. I watch you try to find comfort, in food, in nature, in me, and know it can never be found.

Except, maybe, hopefully, in death.

So kill me before you go.

A Blacksmith's Heart

Conscripted men have a low survival rate. We knew this when the duke rode into town to make the announcement. "All able-bodied men, aged sixteen and up, are to join the king in defending the kingdom!"

The war was on the other side of the kingdom, so he was okay leaving me. A raid on our town was unlikely. Our food stores for the winter might be lower, but not dangerously low. My husband had other worries.

"If I don't come back, how will you pay off the smithy? How will you buy bread?"

"I know Gurtrude at the bakery," I told him. "And I'll pay off the smithy with my work."

He smiled, brushing a tight curl behind my ear. "I sure you could."

"But I don't want to," I said, curling into his chest. "So come back."

I spent every day in the smithy, touching his tools. He'd taught me basic items – nails and horseshoes – and when Gurtrude needed to fix a shelf in the bakery, she learned how to hammer using the nails I struggled to make on my own.

There were no men. We had to do it ourselves. Nails and horseshoes turned into door handles and shelf brackets.

Then came the announcement of the war's end, of our victory. A slow trickle of men came back to town. A third returned, but not my husband. I couldn't bother with the fires or bellows. I couldn't bother with eating.

Gurtrude knocked on my door, soft, and then hard enough to swing it inward. She had a note for me, a reminder of payment for the smithy, and I remembered telling my husband I'd pay it off with my own hands. It was one of the last things I said to him. It was something I'd make true.

That night, I made my first sword. I took the weight of my loneliness and poured it into a broadsword. Took the emptiness of my house and compressed it into a spiked hilt. The sharp pain of the void in my chest became the sword's edge, the coldness of our bed the sting it gave when I cut my finger testing it.

It was large and cold and heavy. It was sharp and uneven and completely unusable, poorly balanced in weight and emotion. I called it the Sword of Darkness.

I couldn't make another sword. I'd hammered out my grief, but it was there, and swords had been my husband's specialty. I returned to household items – plain and useful – until I noticed someone new in town. I looked down the street as I began my walk to Gurtrude's bakery, still run by her as her husband returned missing a hand, and saw a woman on one of the hills outside of town.

She stood there, in the dawn light, looking down at our town, and something in my chest lurched. She was beautiful. She was dainty. She was powerful. She started walking down the path to town and I lost her behind the roofs. I don't remember what I said that morning to Gurtrude, but she will happily tell you how I came up to her window to say "July is a great month" with a dopey smile.

The woman wouldn't leave my head, and I found myself heating metal for a second sword. I tempered the steel so it reminded me of the flash of vermillion light on her brown hair. The thick, heavy pommel was my suddenly beating heart, stretching toward a delicate guard. The faint hope that I might love again, one day, if other people were catching my eye, became its barely-there fuller.

It wasn't a sword to wield damage on the battlefield, the pommel a better bludgeon than the sword's ability to cut. I'd kept the edges thick, uncertain about what the sword would do, uncertain about what to do with a beating heart.

When that woman turned up at the smithy two days later, hoping to have her dagger sharpened, I gave her the sword instead. "The Sword of July Red Morning," I told her. "It's more art than anything, but I want you to have it."

"You're really giving me this?"

"I thought of you while making it, and no one around here will buy it. There are better sword makers a half-day's ride to the south. But I'm the blacksmith for you if you want anything else."

"How 'bout you?" she asked.

Her kiss was as fine as her hair.

The night before my second wedding, I wielded the hammer and anvil a third time. I'd found love again, and it was energizing.

My joy made the sword gleam. The warm leather of the

grip came from her hand in mine. And because I now knew life always had something good waiting for me, the sword edge remained blunt. Joy doesn't cut, even if the memory of my husband bruised me that day.

The Sword of Light, I called it. I hung it on my wall of swords, each arranged point down.

I show off my new ring to any visitor, wedged against my first. Fired clay and hammered iron, love for me on display to the world. But I keep my sword collection private for me and Lucille. They're each full of personal, battered emotions. The cut of grief. The uncertain weight of hope. The warmth of a second love.

I can love. I can lose. And I can love again.

I Like A Little Mystery

You come in every day at three, or sometimes three thirty, and sit in the corner after ordering your drink. You don't look up from your laptop and you sure as hell don't talk to anyone.

Except for me. You have to place your coffee order.

People don't pay attention to you, aside from noting your seat is taken, but I look your way a few times every day and wonder.

On Monday, you're a teacher grading papers your students turned in via e-mail. By your face, I assume most of them suck.

On Tuesday, you're a scientist studying mice. You're concentrating really hard on writing an article to submit for a journal on your latest research.

Wednesday, Wednesday you're a writer. You will never publish, your words are just for you, but you put a lot of effort into it all the same.

Come Thursday, you're a lawyer and you're reviewing past cases as they relate to your current client. Despite your research, you think you'll lose.

And on Friday, you're putting together a budget for the

small business you founded. You smirk a little, so I know you found an investor.

I always say good luck as you leave, calling out from behind the counter. You ignore me, just like everyone else.

But that's okay. It means you cannot break the ritual, or your luck will sour. I smile at your back and look forward to next week.

The Beckoning Future

Taliesin hesitated at the rough-hewn door before him. He had traveled through the winter snows to Camelot not to entertain the kingdom's court, but to meet with the one man in all of Britain who might soothe his dreams.

Yet, Taliesin could not knock on the door to Myrddin's rooms. Why would Britain's greatest sorcerer agree to talk to a simple bard one year past his apprenticeship? Taliesin gathered his courage; he had questions and a warning to deliver.

The door opened before Taliesin raised his fist.

Myrddin stood before him with hair halfway to grey and a face filled with laugh lines. He didn't wear the rich robes he had the night before but rather a plain linen shirt and patched breeches.

The man looked directly at Taliesin and said, "You're a Seer."

Taliesin jumped. "How do you know I'm a Seer?"

Myrddin smiled. "Your performance of the *Vortigern Cycle* last night included previously unsung details."

It was no surprise the man before him had noticed. The *Vortigern Cycle* illustrated Myrddin's first great deed, and the version sung at courts hadn't changed in ten years. Taliesin's rendition, on the other hand, contained scenes he had Seen.

"Do you See often?" Myrddin asked, stepping aside to invite Taliesin into his chambers.

The rooms were simpler than Taliesin expected. Myrddin was, after all, one of King Uther's favored advisors. Taliesin had imagined a large bed with silk covers, elaborately carved wardrobes and desks. What he saw instead was space more akin to a healer's tent. Tables with alchemy equipment, bookshelves holding texts and curiosities, dried herbs hanging from the rafters. One wall contained a crackling hearth. Hidden in a corner, as if only there by necessity, stood a narrow bed and slim wardrobe.

Taliesin might be inside, surrounded by thick stone muffling the earth beneath his feet, but he felt as if he walked into a druid camp in the forest. His nomadic people never settled indoors; they considered Myrddin an oddity for staying in Camelot. But, Taliesin thought, in a place like this, with the scent of herbs, sun, and open windows, his soul could be temporally content.

With a flick of his wrist, Myrddin rotated a hook so the kettle hanging from it swung to hover over the flames in the hearth. "You don't object to a drink?"

"I, you don't have to, my lord," Taliesin sputtered.

"Oh, enough of that. We're kin. People here only call me 'my lord' because Uther's fond of proper etiquette." Myrddin brushed off a table and pulled out a chair for Taliesin to sit before puttering around the room looking for cups.

The kettle whistled. Being a courteous guest, Taliesin

decided to assist Myrddin with his preparations. He focused his power on the kettle.

"*Float to me,*" he commanded. Slowly, it lifted itself off the hook and drifted toward the table. "*Land here gently.*" With a loop of his hands, Taliesin directed the kettle to rest on a pile of cloth before him.

"I see you have more than a bard's level of talent to evoke emotions with words," Myrddin commented, setting down two cups.

Taliesin glowed pink. "It's not as great as yours. To use the power of words without even speaking..." He trailed off, still awed to be in the presence of the older druid. Only after Myrddin placed a cup of mulled wine in his hands did Taliesin realize he had been staring for the last minute. Sheepishly, he hid his gaze behind the clay cup as he took a sip around the floating herbs.

"Now tell me, what brought you to Camelot? Or should I say my door?"

"Seeing. It's a new talent," Taliesin answered. "The dreams started this year while I traveled through Wessex."

"Ah," Myrddin said. "Is King Cenwalh still against magic?"

"He and most of his subjects, now the majority of the kingdom has converted to Christianity. It is difficult to come to terms with a new talent in a realm eager to burn you for it."

"Is that what brought you to Camelot? To learn how to See from me?"

"Yes. And..."

"And?"

"Warn you. Maybe. Myrddin, I only ever See you."

"Me?"

"Yes," Taliesin mumbled into his cup. Some of what he'd seen had been rather risqué and he was hesitant to catch the other man's eyes.

"What do you See?" Myrddin asked, voice gentle.

With a great sigh, Taliesin closed his eyes and brought up the images in his mind. He did not know if it was the Seer's gift or his focused observance that allowed him to remember what he Saw in fine detail. "You, courting a woman. She has copper hair, a willowy body. You talk frequently, about what I do not know. I See in silence. You often walk along a shore, and she wears jewelry with symbols of Avalon. Sometimes the two of you are, ah, *enjoying* each other."

"It's nice to know that one day, I will find love again." Myrddin's smile was evident in his voice.

Taliesin shook his head, eyes still closed. "I See more. You in a cave, beating against the stone. Yelling. Fingertips raw. You try to speak light into being and it sputters."

Though his visions were silent, Taliesin saw the anguish, the betrayal on Myrddin's face. Taliesin suspected the woman would be responsible for locking Myrddin away. Regardless, it was not the question the bard came to have answered.

Looking Myrddin in the eye, Taliesin asked what he had traveled so far to learn. "Can I stop Seeing?"

"You no longer wish to See into the future? It's a useful gift."

"No, I mean..." Taliesin rubbed his forehead, then looked down at the table, embarrassed he had not found an answer himself. "I See you every night. Every time I sleep. I am not bothered by the talent, but I wish to have a proper night's rest. And Seeing you rutting with her is something I don't feel

I should watch." He was certain his face was the same shade of red as Camelot's banners.

Myrddin laughed. "Don't be embarrassed. You've been around the Solstice and Equinox fires, I'm sure. Partaken in a woman or two?"

Yes, but Taliesin had been in reverence of Myrddin forever. He'd rather picture King Uther naked.

"Is it possible for me to control when I See?" Taliesin wanted a reprieve. A solid night's sleep.

Myrddin took a sip of the warmed wine, thinking. "Seeing is a talent few have. As such, little is known about it. Speaking to others who share the talent, I learned each person's embodiment of the gift is unique. Some told me by turning what they See into something that can be read or heard, the visions stop. I believe it has to do with forcing the order and control of language on the raw magic that invades the fluidness of dreams."

"So tonight, I won't See, because I told you what I Saw?"

"It's possible."

Taliesin sighed, relieved. His next question was born out of curiosity rather than need. "Can you See something particular?"

Myrddin looked at him for a long moment before answering. "I have only occasionally managed to See a specific person or place. Only once was I shown exactly what I needed to advise my king. Dreams are difficult to control and Seeing dreams more so."

Taliesin frowned. If the famed Myrddin had problems with Seeing, Taliesin had little hope in controlling the visions. "What helped you guide them?"

Myrddin shot him a grin. "Meditation. Communication with the Triple Goddess. No matter how it manifests, all power comes from the earth. Being in the good graces of its most powerful goddess helps with many things."

Taliesin considered his affinity to be greater with Brighid as opposed to the Morrigan, but certainly, any connection to the earth would help. Later, he'd experiment with Seeing something in particular. For now, he wanted to stop Seeing. He'd pray to his goddess at the hearth. He would also write his visions and hand them to Myrddin. Spoken words, written words, and a request for aid. Certainly, for the first time in months, he would have a dreamless sleep tonight.

"Thank you, Myrddin, for your wisdom."

#####

Deeper and deeper into a tunnel. A glass castle in a cave. A cauldron, blacker than night, glowing with life.
Nine girls breathing on metal.

#####

Three ships sailing through rocky islands. Each full of strong men. Then one ship limping along, manned by seven.

#####

A row of steeds, bred for war. His own hands on a set of reins.
Elders bowing to a man with a crown on his head gleaming.

#####

Taliesin woke slowly. Talking with Myrddin, it seemed, banished images of the other man from his mind. It hadn't stopped him from Seeing others. Quests, past or future, he didn't know, but the glimpses he'd seen had gone by too fast for him to understand. Except for the last vision.

Traveling and music called to Taliesin's soul. He imagined, wanted, his entire life to be a string of visits to castles around Britain singing songs and entraining courts. But his last dream of the night – *armored horses, his hands holding reins* – predicted that one day he'd be in a royal war party.

Taliesin brushed away the concern of war, kingdoms always fought, and instead focused on why *he* would be involved in one. Myrddin said turning visions into words could stop them from appearing, change the state of the magic. Using magic-imbued words, Taliesin could transform a sad woman into a happy one or turn snow into water. Could he use words to change his last vision into something else? He would never believe he had the power to alter history, not if the earth was positive enough in the events to make him See them, but maybe he could erase his involvement, change *his* future.

The war he Saw would happen, of that Taliesin was certain, but it could be fought without him.

He wrote a song about the mounts. Their color, their temperament, matching horse to rider, describing each one he Saw except himself. He sang it for the court that evening and hoped the magic he put into the words made the new version true.

Taliesin didn't See himself in his visions that night. He considered it a partial success because the black cauldron returned. The limping ships returned. And he Saw a new image – a map of Britain on which sat figures representing armies on either side of a place called Camlann. They all filled his chest with the hollow feeling of tragedy.

He would have preferred Myrddin in all his naked. These images featured no one distinct; he had no one to tell, no way to stop them. Worse, he woke with the same feeling of despair as Seeing Myrddin chained in a cave. Taliesin couldn't See everything; he didn't know what happened to the ships that didn't come home or why that glowing, black cauldron filled him with dread. He wanted the feelings out of his head; the sense of danger, loss, and sorrow.

All he had ever desired was to be a bard. Write songs. Perform for beautiful ladies. Travel and experience the world. Instead, Taliesin wondered if this would be his life. Seeing what he didn't want to See.

Who should he tell about the crystal castle in a cave? The sea quest? A battle at Camlann? He wanted simple, normal dreams.

Taliesin knelt on the floor and prayed to Brighid. *Goddess of fire, of healing. Burn away these images from my mind. Keep my life and mind mine.*

Brighid ignored his prayers.

######

A mountain pass, rocky and bare. Two men with similar features fighting, the younger stabbing the older who falls.

######

The older man again, laid on a slab and dressed in finery and a crown. Around him, a court sobs.

######

A map of Britain on a table, figures on the parchment. Men in armor discussing the placement of armies. A scared finger reached out to move a carved horse closer to a spot marked Camlann.

######

Taliesin frowned at the ceiling in the dawn light. Slowly, he raised his right hand to look at his index finger. A scar ran across it between the first and second joints, the result of string snapping on his psaltery while he played. His finger had been the one in the dream, his visions again placing him in the center of a battle.

King Arthur's war.

He had recognized the dead king he Saw. When Taliesin performed for the court, he sat directly in front of the royal table and had a view of both King Uther and Prince Arthur. The Arthur in his dream was older by at least ten years, wearing his father's crown. *There's time,* Taliesin thought, *to make sure I'm not there.*

Thinking it over Taliesin determined that while no clear individual appeared in every vision, they too were about the prince. His previous Seer dreams had all been about a single person – Myrddin. It made sense for these to be as well.

These scenes of danger. Of loss. Sad things, upsetting things. They all belonged to Prince Arthur. Taliesin wanted out them of his head, he wanted to live *his* life and not Myrddin's or Arthur's or any other. Why would magic not let him be?

He should request an audience with the prince, present him with written accounts of what he had Seen and describe them verbally. Telling Myrddin had worked, telling Prince Arthur could –

Could reveal he was a Seer to the Prince of Camelot. Reveal that, in one of the visions, Taliesin rode with him and in another stood in a war tent. Did he also sail on one of those three ships, two of which were lost? Would he witness the nine maidens blowing on a cauldron that filled him with unease? When war came, did he trade his psaltery for a dagger, or bow, or sword, forsaking the druidic ways of peace?

He needed to see Myrddin.

######

Arms full of tied scrolls, Taliesin knocked on Myrddin's door with his foot, praying the man was home. Thankfully, the door opened.

"Taliesin, how nice of you to visit! What has you looking so troubled?"

Taliesin looked down at the parchments he carried. "I find myself worried about my own life," Taliesin admitted. "I hoped you could help?"

"Of course, come in, come in."

Both men sat at the table, Myrddin directing a pitcher to pour them drinks.

"Myrddin, I need -"

"Hush." The older Druid pushed a cup of watered wine into Taliesin's hand, causing the bard to drop his scrolls. They flittered to the floor.

Taliesin gave him an affronted look. "That's - "

"The cause of your stress. I'm removing it." Myrddin

shoved the air as if pushing a reluctant child out of the house. Taliesin's chair scooted closer to the table, knocking Taliesin's elbow against the edge, and the scattered parchment on the floor swept into a pile out of reach under Myrddin's seat.

"But -"

"Drink."

Sighing, Taliesin did as ordered and let Myrddin pull him into a conversation concerning Myrddin's research. The older Druid was testing different tinctures' effectiveness in curing post-feast headaches.

Taliesin had never been a healer, with words or herbs, but he knew herb lore. Bards traveled; they had to know how to use what the earth produced to flavor food and address minor ailments. And what to avoid to prevent poisoning. He felt pleased he could follow Myrddin's process and learned more about the uses of yarrow.

Hours later, the golden light of sunset streaming through the windows, Taliesin felt more relaxed than he had in days.

"Now," Myrddin said, scooping air with his right hand. The pile of rolled-up parchment under his chair moved to the table. "What has you so worried? Seeing again?"

"Is the future set in stone?"

Myrddin sighed. Taliesin sensed he wished for more wine. "Most of what I Saw came to pass. Maybe not in the same way, but it happened. Rarely do I See an event that doesn't occur."

"So it's possible what I See won't happen?"

"Yes. But it probably will."

Taliesin grimaced and gestured to the parchment pile. As the Myrddin unrolled a scroll, Taliesin explained. "Since talking to you before, all I have Seen are foretellings of tragedy. Costly quests. War. And what I believe is Prince Arthur's death, years into the future."

"You should tell him."

"Me?" Taliesin laughed. "I may have more than a bard's level of word magic, but no one here knows that. I doubt the prince will not grant me an audience, and most of what I See comes to pass after King Uther dies. I ask that you give these descriptions of what I have seen to him. If he reads them, I hope it stops me from seeing his death every night."

"No. You should be the one to tell him and you need to stay."

"Stay?" Taliesin balked at the idea. Despite the weather, he couldn't imagine staying. He missed the smell of the woods, the wide-reaching effect of a strong gust of wind. "I don't want to stay in Camelot. I've had enough of stone walls." Taliesin shook his head. "I *will* leave."

"It's winter. Most bards remain with a single court until the snow thaws. If you're fleeing visions, you need to share them – "

"I will not be you!" Taliesin sank back in his chair, bringing a hand to his face ashamed of his anger. "I will not be you," he said again, softer. "If either Arthur or Uther learn it is I who Sees this, I worry they will keep me at court. I do not want that, Myrddin. I have never desired anything other than the life of a *bard*. I want no part of court life. I want no part in those visions." He jabbed a finger at the pile of scrolls on the table. "They will happen, and I will not be here. I *will not*."

Taliesin swallowed. In the visions he appeared, he excluded himself in its written account. If the magic of the world made Taliesin's visions fixate on Prince Arthur because of his own involvement, both Arthur and his father would want Taliesin close to hear future visions. He'd be forced to give up what he loved, to join Camelot's court. He'd no longer travel, whistle with birds, and sleep beneath the stars. The castle's walls would lean in and squeeze him. Myrddin might be able to live here, but Taliesin couldn't.

"I will not be trapped here," Taliesin insisted again. "I will play once more for the court tonight. They expect it. But I leave early in the morning."

Myrddin frowned. "I assume you want me to give these scrolls to Arthur to read? Declare them as things I Saw?"

"Please, have him read them," Taliesin said, "but you don't have to claim they are yours. I only ask you to keep my name secret."

"If you are trying to prevent something, Taliesin," Myrddin shook his head, "This won't work."

#######

Taliesin woke before dawn, shaking from a vision. He'd Seen the first scene that had unsettled him, the one he thought he had avoided: his own hands on the reins of a horse. His steed was one of several, all supporting men lined up next to Prince Arthur. Then the scene had morphed into a battlefield, the grass slick with blood and at least two of the knights felled by enemy swords.

A pit opened in Taliesin's stomach as he packed, his hands trembling. Removing himself from the song of horses hadn't worked. Would he have to witness those deaths in real life, complete with the added senses of sound and smell? Would he spend his days wondering *is this the day a tragedy happens?*

The image, even if he never Saw the battle again, would haunt him and make his guts churn. He had to leave Camelot behind. He refused to be tied to Prince Arthur.

A knock sounded on his door. He stared at the wood, not sure who else woke this early, before hurrying to answer.

On the other side stood Myrddin. In touch with the earth, those with magic often roused with the sun. No doubt, the older man had risen and immediately made his way to Taliesin's guest chambers.

"Good morning," Myrddin greeted. "Are you packed? I'll walk you to the gate."

Only yawning servants moved about the castle and none bothered the two men. The town bustled with more activity; bakers putting in the first loaf of the day, blacksmiths starting the forges. Myrddin insisted on buying Taliesin breakfast, which they ate companionably while heading to the South Gate.

"I'll see you soon," Myrddin said when they reached the gate.

"I'm not planning on returning," Taliesin said.

Myrddin smiled. "Just as what you Saw of me drew you to Camelot, what you See of Prince Arthur will pull you back here."

"I doubt it."

Myrddin hummed. "Do you know when I'll meet the lady you Saw me with?"

A lady who would be Myrddin's lover, before betraying him to trap him in a cave. King Uther would lose Myrddin's counsel, Camelot its magical protector. No one would ever compare to Myrddin, not in all of history. Camelot's enemies who worried about the sorcerer's powers would have nothing to deter an attack; Arthur had a difficult reign as king before him.

"You'll be back in two years," Myrddin declared.

The weight behind the words crushed Taliesin's heart. Prediction. Certainty. Myrddin had Seen something and the possibilities made Taliesin turn on his heel, leaving Camelot with long, quick strides.

He was a bard. All he ever wanted to be.

Taliesin feared he would be much more.

Please Review

Thank you so much for reading Fae Dreams! If you could do me a favor, please leave a rating or review?

Reviews are extremely important for any book but for indie books like this, they are crucial. Reviews help potential readers discover new books and determine if a book is right for them. They also help authors by increasing exposure, showing the author their work is appreciated, and can serve as a guide to improve future books.

I'd really appreciate it if you took a minute to write a review of Fae Dreams. Doesn't have to be long, maybe tell future readers your favorite story or let them know some of these are short. Even an emoji string would work! Every review makes a difference.

Publication Notes

Many of these stories were originally published on my Tumblr, gwen-tolios, several of which were responses to the public prompts shared by the account writing-prompts.

About the Author

Gwen Tolios is a queer Chicago-based author, staring at Excel sheets by day and writing at night while trying to coax her cat to cuddle. While she got her start in short stories, Gwen has also written fantasy novelettes for children and romances for adults.

For social media links and more, visit https://linktr.ee/gwentolios

STAY IN THE LOOP

Sign up below to receive monthly updates on writing projects and book recs. https://gwentolios.substack.com/